THE

ENCHANTED
TUNNEL

—— BOOK FOUR ——

WANDERING IN THE
WILDERNESS

THE ENCHANTED TUNNEL

BOOK FOUR
WANDERING IN THE WILDERNESS

Marianne Monson

Illustrated by Dan Burr

DESERET
BOOK

SALT LAKE CITY, UTAH

Library of Congress Cataloging-in-Publication Data

Monson, Marianne, 1975– author.
  Wandering in the wilderness / Marianne Monson ; illustrated by Dan Burr.
      p. cm. — (Enchanted tunnel series book 4)
  Summary: Aria and Nathan return to the Enchanted Tunnel and soon find themselves in Book of Mormon times, with Lehi and his family, wandering in the wilderness.
  ISBN 978-1-60908-069-3 (paperbound)
  1. Space and time—Juvenile fiction.   2. Book of Mormon—Juvenile fiction.   3. Nephi (Book of Mormon figure)—Juvenile fiction.   4. Lehi (Book of Mormon figure)—Juvenile fiction.   5. Mormons—Juvenile fiction.   6. Brothers and sisters—Juvenile fiction.   [1. Space and time—Fiction.   2. Book of Mormon—Fiction.   3. Nephi (Book of Mormon figure)—Fiction.   4. Lehi (Book of Mormon figure)—Fiction.   5. Mormons—Fiction.   6. Brothers and sisters—Fiction.   7. Twins—Fiction.]   I. Burr, Dan, 1951– illustrator.   II. Title.   III. Series: Monson, Marianne, 1975– Enchanted tunnel series ; book 4.
  PZ7.M76282Wan 2011
  [Fic]—dc22   2010048979

Printed in the United States of America
Malloy Lithographing Incorporated, Ann Arbor, MI

10   9   8   7   6   5   4   3   2   1

For my brothers,
Benjamin and Jordan

A BIG THANK-YOU

Special thanks to Dr. Jeffrey Chadwick, professor of archaeology and Near Eastern studies at Brigham Young University, for his invaluable knowledge of the history and region, which he so willingly shared with me.

Thanks also to Nasser, who arranged for the opportunity to experience a Bedouin tent dinner at the BYU Jerusalem Center.

A NOTE TO THE READER

When I read a good book, I like to know if it *really* happened. The Enchanted Tunnel books are historical fiction, which means that part of the book is true and part is made up. Nathan and Aria and their adventures in the enchanted tunnel are imagined.

But the information that comes from the scriptures and church history is absolutely true. It *really* happened. We know about these events from the scriptures, pioneer journals, and historical records. Some of the details, such as what the characters were eating or doing on a specific day, are invented, but only after learning about the types of things they *often* did.

When I was a child, I sometimes found it

difficult to relate to people in the scriptures who lived long ago. Luckily, I had teachers and parents who brought the scriptures to life. These teachers opened a magic tunnel in my mind that helped me imagine myself in the story. It is my hope that the Enchanted Tunnel books will do the same for you.

1

CARVING CAMELS

"This is hard!" said Nathan. His face twisted with the effort of moving the knife across the wood.

"Yeah," agreed Brother King. "It is. Imagine if this were the only way you had to make furniture or tools for your family."

"My mom would be in trouble," said Nathan, grinning up at his favorite Primary teacher, who was helping out the regular Cub Scout leader.

Brother King tousled Nathan's hair. "You're very resourceful, Nathan. I bet you'd figure something out." He showed Nathan how to hold the knife at a slightly different angle to make cutting easier. The lump of wood didn't look very much like the camel Nathan had pictured in his mind.

While Nathan continued working on his project, Brother King told the Cubs about the types of wood that worked best for carving. He showed them pictures from the Scout pamphlet. "Soft woods like fir are easier to cut," Brother King explained. "But if you need something to be sturdy, you have to use a hard, springy wood like hickory or yew."

Nathan glanced up at the picture. The tree looked a little like one that grew in his backyard.

Nathan's Scout leader thanked Brother King for coming to help with the wood projects. "Keep working at them," said Brother King. "In no time you'll have your Whittling Chip Card."

Nathan looked down at the lumpy, misshapen piece of wood in his hands. He kind of doubted he'd get that award very soon. It didn't seem like this was his talent.

Brother King stopped by Nathan's chair again before he left. "Been doing any more research lately, Nathan?" he asked.

"I learned a lot about the temple in Jerusalem!" said Nathan. "Did you know it was enormous, and people cooked animals in the middle and danced and wore black prayer boxes on their heads?"

"Really?" said Brother King, shaking his head and laughing. "I didn't know that."

"Yeah," said Nathan, "and Jesus taught there when he was only twelve."

Brother King smiled. "I wish I could get every kid in the class as excited about the scriptures as you've been lately. What are you going to learn about next?"

Nathan's face lit up. "I don't know," he said, "but I can't wait to find out!"

Brother King laughed again. "Well, tell me when you decide," he said.

"Don't worry, I will," said Nathan.

As Brother King waved good-bye, Nathan couldn't help thinking about the enchanted tunnel. Where *would* it take them next? He was ready for another adventure. Nathan wiped off the tools he had been using and returned them to his Cub Scout leader.

"Are you finished?" asked his leader.

"Yeah," said Nathan. "I just remembered I have to do something."

"Don't forget your pocketknife," said the leader.

Nathan grabbed the camel-shaped lump of wood and his knife, making sure it was locked shut, and then called good-bye to his friends.

2

LET'S GO!

Nathan walked carefully out of the Primary room, but as soon as he was out of sight, he dashed to the door, flung it open, and raced through the parking lot to his house across the street. The light was on in Aria's room on the ground floor. Without bothering to go inside, he knocked on her window.

The curtain moved aside and a surprised Aria looked out at him.

Nathan motioned for her to open the window. She unlocked it and gaped at him. "What are you *doing?*" she asked.

"Let's go through the tunnel!" said Nathan.

"Right *now?*" said Aria. "I thought you were at Scouts."

"I was, silly, so that means the church is open. My Cub meeting is just about over anyway, and it will seem like we're gone for only a minute."

Aria put down the book she had been reading. Her eyes shone with excitement. "Okay," she said. "I'll come. Just a minute. Do you have your stuff?"

"Can you grab my scripture bag from my room?" said Nathan. "It's all ready to go."

Aria shut the window and grabbed the tunnel clothes from her closet. She walked into the hallway. "Mom!" she called. "Is it okay if I go pick up Nathan from Scouts at the church?"

"Sure, honey," said Mom. "That's sweet of you. When you get back, I'll have dinner ready."

"Okay," said Aria. She grabbed the scripture bag from Nathan's room, put the tunnel clothes into a sack, and opened the back door. In the yard, Nathan danced with excitement.

"C'mon, let's go!" he said.

Aria handed him the scripture bag, and Nathan added his pocketknife and camel lump to the bag. The twins dashed across the parking lot to the church building.

When they got there, they slipped inside.

"Where should we change?" said Aria.

"The restrooms?" asked Nathan.

They went into the restrooms, clutching their costumes. Aria tugged off her T-shirt and slipped the long, brown, dresslike costume over her head. She put her tennis shoes back on even though they didn't match with her costume very well. So far, all the scripture stories they had visited seemed to involve a lot of walking!

She met up with Nathan in the hall. He was wearing a pioneer costume, and he was holding a cream-colored shawl, just in case. "Let's go," said Nathan.

They walked toward the cultural hall. Just then a group of Scouts came around the corner.

"Nathan?" said one boy.

"What are you *wearing?*" asked another.

"Uhh . . . uhh . . . ," said Nathan, his face turning bright pink. *Why couldn't he think of anything to say?*

"We have to practice a skit!" said Aria, dragging him toward the gym. "Gotta go!"

The Scouts snickered and called after them. "Have fun, Nathan!"

Nathan pulled away from Aria's grasp. "A skit practice?" he asked. "With *you?*"

"Well, you weren't saying anything!" said Aria. "What did you want me to say?"

"I dunno," said Nathan. "Something cool like . . ."

"Oh, like, 'We found an enchanted tunnel, wanna come see?'"

"No," grumbled Nathan, "not that."

"I guess we need to decide what to say," said Aria.

"How about 'My grandma forced me to wear this,'" said Nathan.

"Something like that." Aria smiled. She pulled a faded, patched bonnet from the bottom of the sack. "Don't worry about them," she said. "Imagine how jealous they would be if they knew where we were really going!"

"*We* don't know where we're going," said Nathan, still a little grumpy.

"But we're going to find out!" said Aria. She tied on the bonnet as they entered the cultural hall. She went straight to the storage cupboard under the stairs and opened the cupboard door. The rack of chairs had been moved out, luckily. Nathan knelt down and began to crawl. Aria came right behind him.

Zing! An electric shock passed through the tunnel and Nathan's fingers tingled.

"It's working," he said.

Soon the smooth concrete floor of the cupboard changed into rocky tunnel ground. There was a bright, blinding light at the end.

3

DESERT WARRIORS

Aria crept to the entrance of the tunnel, listening for noises, but it was very quiet outside the cave. She peered out. No wonder it was so bright—they were looking straight into the morning sun.

"Where are we?" asked Nathan.

"On top of a hill, I think," said Aria. They were on a rocky ridge. A cluster of small scrubby trees grew together near the entrance of the cave. Nathan noticed the trees and thought of the woodworking class he had just finished. He wondered what kind of trees they were. The rest of the ridge was barren and stony.

"Where is everyone?" asked Nathan. The

hill was completely silent, with no sign of life in sight.

"I don't know," said Aria. "Maybe we should go look around." There weren't any trails on the hill, but they followed the curve of the land. Nathan jumped off a rock. Aria knelt down to watch a beetle digging in the dirt. When she glanced back up, a lizard slipped out of sight behind a stone.

"This is a desert," said Aria. "Do you think there might be snakes?"

"Probably," said Nathan, picking up a rock. "And scorpions."

Aria shivered. "Why are so many scripture stories set in the desert?" she asked as they started making their way down the hill. There was still no sign of people. She was starting to wonder what they were possibly going to do here. "Can you check the GPS and figure out where we are?" she asked Nathan.

Nathan started to pull the GPS out of his scripture bag. He stopped and put a finger to his mouth. "Shhh," said Nathan. "Did you hear that?"

Aria listened. A voice whooped and hollered a war cry. Another voice joined in. The voices sounded as though they were coming straight toward them. Aria glanced around for somewhere to hide, when she heard the sounds of scuffling just around a bend in the hillside.

Aria darted behind a rock as two young boys chased each other into the clearing. "Yarahhh!" one cried.

"Zazooom!" shouted another. The older of the two boys carried a small bow that he pointed straight at Aria. He had a miniature quiver of arrows slung across his back. The other boy held an empty slingshot that he spun in a circle over his head.

"Aahh!" cried Aria, crouching behind the rock. Nathan tried to follow her, still dragging the scripture bag.

The boys stopped in confusion when they saw Nathan and Aria. Aria peeked out from behind her hiding spot. "Oh, they're just little kids," she said with a sigh of relief.

The boy with the slingshot started laughing when he saw Aria's worried look. He started jabbering to the other boy, nudging him and pointing.

The older boy, who had been aiming the bow, glared at the one who was laughing. He beckoned to Nathan and Aria, as if telling them it would be all right. *"Za be'seder,"* he said, smiling encouragingly. *"Bohu he'na."*

Nathan fumbled with the GPS, which he knew would translate what they were saying. He finally found the switch and turned it on.

"Ani matz'er . . . sorry we scared you," said

the older boy. "We were only playing. Are you all right?"

"Yeah," said Aria, coming out from behind the rock, brushing her dress. "We're okay— you just surprised us."

Nathan came forward to meet the boys. They were a lot smaller than they had sounded. The older boy looked like he was maybe seven, and the younger was around five. "Your hunting cries were really good," said Nathan.

"Thanks," said the older boy, smiling and nudging the other. "Our older brothers taught us. They are hunting right now. I am Jacob, and this is Joseph." He nodded to the younger boy. The brothers were wearing dusty worn robes and leather sandals on their feet. They had fabric wound around their heads.

"I'm Nathan. This is Aria," said Nathan. "Can we come with you?"

"Sure," said Jacob. "Do you have a bow?"

17

When Nathan shook his head, Jacob handed him his. "Wow!" said Nathan. "Thanks!" The wood was curved and springy when he pulled on the string.

"Let's go!" shouted Joseph, who handed his slingshot to Aria.

"Thanks," said Aria, giving it a twirl.

Joseph and Jacob set off down the side of the hill. They whooped and hollered, as they jumped off the rocks.

"Aren't you supposed to be quiet when you go hunting?" asked Aria.

Nathan shrugged. He aimed the arrowless bow into the trees and let out a cry.

"Did you figure out where we are?" asked Aria.

Nathan looked at the GPS. "It says Arabian Peninsula."

"Arabia?" said Aria. "We're in *Arabia?* I don't remember any scripture stories set there."

"I don't know," said Nathan, "but this is fun!" He shoved the GPS back into the bag and picked up the bow again. He set off after Jacob and Joseph, trying to holler like they did.

Aria picked up the slingshot and followed after the boys. *I wonder what they are hunting for,* she thought. *Probably not lizards.*

The small party of children wound their way across the hill. The morning sun made long shadows in the valleys. From here, Aria could see the hills that descended to a low plain and a dark blue patch of sea below.

She followed the boys, swinging the slingshot over her head. She thought it would probably be hard to actually hit something with it.

The boys were calling louder now. *Maybe they have found something,* thought Aria. She hurried forward to see what it was. In the middle of the circle of boys stood a young man holding a large metal bow. He was dressed simply, in fabric that was tied around his waist. A white headscarf protected his head and shoulders from the sun and desert sand.

Joseph and Jacob jumped and clamored around him. "Did you get something?" asked Joseph.

"Can we help now?" begged Jacob.

The young man's eyes looked sad, but he smiled at the boys. "My two favorite hunters," he said. "No, I didn't get anything." He shook his head. "I'm afraid the others won't be too happy with me." He held up the bow. "My bow is broken."

"Oh, no!" said Joseph. "Your bow is the best one."

The man nodded.

Jacob jumped up and down. "It's okay, we still have mine!"

The man smiled sadly. "I don't think we're

going to be able to feed all the hungry mouths at camp with your bow, Jacob," he said. "Who are your friends?" he asked.

"This is Nathan and Aria," Joseph said. "They're helping us." He pointed at the man as he spoke to the children. "This is our big brother Nephi."

4

WHAT DO YOU SAY TO NEPHI?

Nathan just stood there with his mouth hanging open. Aria gasped. *Nephi? In Arabia?* Suddenly she remembered the story of Nephi's broken bow in the wilderness. "Oh . . . hi," she said at last. She felt self-conscious being so close to such a great prophet.

Nephi looked at them both curiously. "Are you camped around here?" he asked.

"Umm . . . sort of," said Aria, wondering what to say. "Joseph and Jacob were just teaching us how to hunt."

Nephi smiled. "Well, usually when you hunt, you want to be quiet so you don't scare the animals. Joseph and Jacob have their own . . . special technique." He tousled Jacob's hair.

"Told you," Aria mouthed to Nathan. Nathan rolled his eyes.

Just then, two other young men walked into the clearing. They also carried bows, but theirs were made of wood. "Nephi!" called one. "Did you get anything?"

Nephi shook his head. "My bow broke, Laman. It will be of no use to us."

"*What?*" said Laman. "How could you be so foolish? That bow has kept us alive."

The other man, who Aria guessed to be Lemuel, said, "We will return to camp empty-handed, then, to our hungry wives and children. Our bows have lost their spring."

"It's this wretched climate," said Laman. "Nothing can survive in it. Was *this* in your dream, Nephi?" His face was dark and angry.

"The Lord will provide for us, Lemuel," said Nephi.

Lemuel grumbled a response, but Aria

couldn't understand what he had said. "Come on," said Laman. "Let's go back to camp. The dreamer is out of ideas. It's time for the real men to take care of their families."

Lemuel followed Laman down the steep, rocky ravine. They didn't glance back to see if anyone else was following.

"What are we going to do, Nephi?" asked Jacob. Joseph looked as though he were about to cry.

Nephi watched his brothers walking away. His eyes were filled with sorrow. "I'm not really sure, Jacob," he said. "But I know the Lord didn't bring us here to starve. Something will work out."

"Can't you use my bow?" asked Jacob.

Nephi shook his head. "It's just not big enough," he replied. "Why don't all of you head back to camp? I'm going to stay here and say a prayer."

"Can we pray with you?" asked Joseph.

"Do you want to?" asked Nephi.

Aria nodded.

"Me too," said Nathan.

"Okay," said Nephi. They circled together, and Nephi clasped his hands. Aria closed her eyes and listened to Nephi's words as he pled with the Lord to help them find food to feed their wives and children. Her heart felt calm, and she knew that the Lord would help them. Nephi finished the prayer, and they all said, "Amen."

Nephi was quiet for a moment after the prayer. "I think we need some wood," he said at last. "But it will be very difficult to find in this desert."

Nathan thought about what Nephi had said. Suddenly he remembered the scraggly trees they had seen by the entrance to the cave.

"I know where you can find some wood!" said Nathan.

"You do?" Nephi asked, raising his eyebrows.

"Yes!" said Nathan. "We saw some trees before we met Jacob and Joseph."

"That's right!" Aria nodded.

"Do you think you can lead us back to that spot?" asked Nephi.

"Definitely!" said Nathan. "It's this way." He scampered down the ravine and then turned back up the hill, retracing their steps. Joseph and Jacob galloped after them, whooping and hollering.

When they got to the place where they had met Joseph and Jacob, Aria pointed. "That's where I hid because I thought we were being attacked," she said.

Nephi smiled. "My little brothers sound a little like a desert war party."

"It's just up here," said Nathan, pointing up the hill. They began to climb the rocks, but the sun had risen in the sky and it was much hotter now. Sweat glistened on Nathan's forehead. He led them to the top of the ridge. In a sheltered nook lay the entrance to the tunnel. Scraggly trees grew alongside, protected by the walls of rock.

"Will this work?" asked Nathan.

Nephi grinned. "It's a good thing my brothers found you," he said. "We hunted all day yesterday and didn't find any wood like this. These are acacia trees, and they have strong, springy wood—perfect for making bows. They are rare and difficult to find in the desert."

Nathan and Aria looked at each other. Aria didn't know how the enchanted tunnel worked, but she was pretty sure it hadn't been an accident that they had ended up right next to those trees.

Nephi tested a few branches before selecting a long, springy one for the bow and several smaller branches for arrows. Nathan pulled out his pocketknife and helped cut off the smaller branches, being careful to cut away from himself just as Brother King had shown him. Joseph and Jacob held the small branches and pretended to have a sword fight.

Underneath the trees, dry dead wood lay scattered about on the ground. "We should gather that to use for firewood," said Nephi. Aria gathered the wood into a big pile.

"Thanks for your help," said Nephi when they were finished. "This wood will make a great bow. Are you ready to head back to camp?"

"Do we have to?" asked Joseph.

Nephi smiled. "There are probably going to

be a lot of hungry, grumpy people there," he agreed. "But we have to face them sooner or later. Besides, how could they be upset when they see they have such excellent hunters watching out for them?"

Joseph grinned. "Wahoo!" he yelled, setting off down the hill, swinging his slingshot around his head. Jacob scampered quickly after his brother. Nathan picked up some of the firewood and ran after the boys.

Aria collected more wood, and Nephi picked up the pieces for the bow. They followed the boys down the hill.

Aria was a little shy about talking to Nephi, but he was very kind, and when he smiled, his eyes sparkled. Before finding the enchanted tunnel she had always thought of prophets as being very solemn and serious, but Nephi laughed and even joked around. He reminded

Aria of her own father, and she felt a twinge of longing for her dad.

Nephi spoke of his wife and said that she was going to have a child soon. He talked of Jerusalem, his home.

"I've been to Jerusalem too," said Aria.

"The temple in Jerusalem is very sacred. I believe we will build a new temple when we arrive in the land where the Lord is leading us," said Nephi.

They left the hills behind and walked across flat ground leading down to the water's edge. The water sparkled in the sunshine as far as they could see. "That's the Red Sea," said Nephi. "The sea where Moses led the children of Israel. My brothers are not the first to complain about wandering in the wilderness."

Ahead of them now, Aria could see the camp. A line of flat-topped tents hung with brightly colored woven blankets was pitched in a cluster several yards from the water. Children ran around playing, while a group of women washed clothes in the water. Other women were weaving fabrics and grinding seeds between stones.

"Nephi!" called a woman as they passed the first tent. The woman, who must have been his wife, hurried toward him. Her hair was bound with a red striped scarf, and she wore a black dress covered with bright embroidery. Her dark eyes shone. "I've been worried about you," she said.

Nephi touched her shoulder gently. "Did Laman tell you about my bow, Huldah?"

"He told everyone about it," said his wife. "Even your father is complaining."

Nephi looked shocked. "My father?"

Huldah nodded.

"I must speak to him," said Nephi. He put the wood for the bow inside the tent and

headed toward the largest tent, which was located in the center of the camp.

Aria trailed behind, not wanting to be in the way. Nathan joined her, along with Joseph and Jacob, whose faces were serious. A group of men was waiting for Nephi. They called to him angrily, and Aria could see the gloomy face of Laman, his finger pointing accusingly at Nephi.

The other men surrounded him, and Aria heard Nephi's voice trying to calm them down. Joseph looked like he wanted to cry again, and Jacob's shoulders slumped. He drew in the dirt with one of the arrow sticks.

5

BOW-MAKING LESSONS

After several minutes, Nephi left the group and returned to his own tent. The kids watched as he picked up the wood he had left there and gathered some tools from the tent.

"Do you think he'll let us help?" asked Nathan.

"I think so," said Jacob. "The others seemed really angry, but Nephi usually lets us come along."

Nathan pulled out his pocketknife, and Aria picked up the arrow sticks she had carried.

When they reached Nephi, Aria said, "Don't worry, Nephi, we'll work with you."

Nephi looked up and smiled, even though Aria thought his soft, brown eyes still looked sad. "I'd love that. It seems that plenty of people want to talk, but helpers are harder to find."

"I have this knife if you want to use it," said Nathan, holding up his pocketknife.

"Amazing," said Nephi, "that looks very useful! Usually making a bow and arrow takes several days, but we don't have much time, so this is going to have to be quick. A knife like that will speed things up." He held the knife and looked at it curiously.

"What can we do?" asked Aria.

"Can you smooth out the sticks for the arrows?" asked Nephi.

"Sure!" said Nathan and Aria at once.

Nathan showed Aria the technique Brother King had used at the Scout activity. "You hold the knife like this," he explained.

"Like this?" she asked. Nathan nodded.

Jacob and Joseph pulled off the twigs, and

Nathan and Aria used the knife to remove the bumps until the sticks were smooth and straight.

Meanwhile, Nephi was forming the bow with some metal tools. When he had the correct shape, he used rough stones to sand the wood. Nathan thought about all the tools they'd had at the Cub meeting and wished he had brought some with him.

"How are those arrows coming?" Nephi asked. They held up the smooth sticks. "Perfect!" said Nephi. "Now we need to find some sharp rocks for the ends."

They set off to search around the camp for sharp, pointed stones. Aria searched along the shoreline of the Red Sea. The afternoon sun beat down upon her head, and the cool blue water felt heavenly as it washed over her toes. She looked at the sun glinting on the surface of the water. Right next to the water, a triangular

shape glinted. She scooped it up. "I found one!" she called.

"Me too!" said Nathan.

Aria collected several more sharp, triangular-shaped stones and returned to where the other boys had gathered. They all held out their hands.

"We have enough," said Nathan. "Let's go!"

When they got back to Nephi, he used Nathan's knife to cut a notch at each end of the arrows. He also cut a notch in the top and bottom of the bow.

"What will you use for string?" asked Nathan.

"String?" said Nephi. "The bow is finished with tendon fibers." He showed them a loop that looked like glossy twine. He tied one end to the top of the bow, pulled it taut across the bottom, and then tied it tightly.

They cut notches in the arrow sticks and

fitted the stones inside the notches, binding them with more fiber.

When they were finished, Nephi lifted the bow and arrows proudly. "Excellent work," he said. "I couldn't have done it without you!"

"Where are you going to go hunt?" asked Joseph.

"That is a very good question," said Nephi. "We didn't see any game yesterday, which is partly why my brothers are upset. They are afraid there is nothing to find. Unless you want lizards for dinner, of course."

Aria grimaced.

"Yuck," said Nathan.

"We've eaten worse on this journey," said Nephi. "But it would take a lot of lizards to feed this family. I think I will ask my father for help," he said.

"Your father was upset, wasn't he?" asked

Aria. She remembered the angry crowd that had gathered around Nephi.

Nephi nodded. "Yes, but he's still my father." He put the bow over his shoulder and turned back toward the large tent again. The kids trailed after him, wondering what to do now.

When Nephi arrived at the tent, he called, "Father?" A blanket was moved aside so Nephi could enter. Aria could hear voices conversing, and a few minutes later it seemed she could hear a man weeping.

At last the blanket covering the door of the tent was pushed aside. A man in a long red robe stepped out. He had white hair and a flowing white beard. In his hands he held a golden ball and his cheeks glistened. Aria knew this must be the prophet Lehi.

"Children!" he called. "Come here!" In response to his call, several men and women gathered around the door to his tent. Nathan, Aria, Joseph, and Jacob came closer.

Nephi followed his father out of the tent. He too looked as though he might have been crying. Aria looked at the people gathered around the white-haired man. Their faces looked worn and exhausted. She couldn't imagine the journey they had survived.

"I have just finished speaking with Nephi," Lehi explained. "He wanted to seek the Lord's direction in deciding where to look for food." His eyes were piercing and sought out each person in the crowd. Aria felt as though he could look right into her heart if he wanted to.

"After humbling myself and repenting of my murmuring, I am ready to consult with the Lord. I ask for your faith and prayers."

An older woman wearing a blue scarf moved closer to her husband. He smiled kindly at her.

That must be Sariah, Aria thought. Huldah came and stood by Nephi's side.

Lehi closed his eyes and offered a prayer seeking the Lord's direction and asking Him to guide Nephi to find food. A familiar burning in Aria's chest let her know the Spirit was there.

When Lehi finished the prayer, he opened his eyes, expecting the needles on the ball to move. To everyone's surprise, the Liahona now had a circle of scrolling engraved all around the edge.

"That wasn't there before, was it?" whispered Nathan. Aria shook her head.

Lehi read the scrolling words, and his arms began to tremble. He cleared his throat and said, "This new writing says that the pointers in the ball work according to our own faith and diligence." His voice shook as he continued. "If we are obedient, the Liahona will guide us. If not, we will be left alone in this wilderness."

43

A quiet murmur broke out in the crowd that had gathered. Some shook their heads. Others nodded in agreement. Many looked frightened.

"That's the Liahona," said Aria to Nathan. "The *real* Liahona." Nathan nodded solemnly.

Lehi closed his eyes. He looked deeply shaken. Sariah placed a hand upon his shoulder. "We need the Lord's guidance," said Lehi, opening his eyes. "Let us stay humble and have faith. The Lord knows where we are going."

Nephi took the compass from his father. He looked solemn.

As most of the men and women turned back to their own tents, Aria and Nathan approached Nephi hesitantly. "Would you like to see?" Nephi asked.

Aria nodded. Nephi lowered his hands, gently cupping the precious treasure. The ball was golden and intricately carved. Two needles

pointed in a straight direction to the mountain directly behind them. Around the edge of the ball, scrolling letters were engraved. Aria reached out and ran one finger across the letters.

Nephi gave the ball back to Lehi and put his hand upon Lehi's shoulder. "Father, I'm going to the top of the mountain, as the compass directs."

"Thank you, my son, for your example, even when all those around you are losing faith."

Nephi's arm encircled his father's shoulder as they embraced. Then Nephi pulled his bow over his shoulder once more.

"May we come?" asked Joseph.

Nephi shook his head. "I couldn't have made the bow without you, but I need to travel quickly to find meat before nightfall, if

the Lord is willing. Will you stay here and pro-
tect the camp?"

"Can't we help?" asked Nathan.

"Yes," said Nephi. "You can have faith that
the Lord will answer our prayers. That is a
huge help. Can you do that?"

"Sure," said Nathan.

Aria nodded.

"Yes! Yes!" said Joseph and Jacob.

"Then we will depend on you," said Nephi.
He waved as he turned to walk away, facing
the mountain ahead of him.

6

WHAT IS FAITH?

Nathan and Aria waved until Nephi was out of sight. Then they sat down by Joseph and Jacob in the middle of camp.

"I'm hungry," said Joseph, rubbing his tummy.

"I hope Nephi finds something really big!" said Jacob.

"Now we just have to wait," said Nathan. He sighed. Waiting was really boring compared to making a bow and arrow. "I wish we could help some other way."

Aria drew in the dirt with her finger. She thought about how Nephi had said they could help by having faith. They had just had a lesson in Primary about faith. "Hey, Nathan," said

Aria. "Do you remember what Brother King said about having faith?"

"Um, I dunno," said Nathan. "Believing something is true."

"Yeah," said Aria, "but he also said that true faith leads to action."

"Oh, yeah, I remember that," said Nathan. "But Nephi told us to wait and have faith."

"But if having faith is acting, then maybe we should do something here to help."

"Like what?" asked Nathan.

"I don't know," said Aria. "But I guess if we believe that Nephi is really going to get meat, then we should help get things ready for when he brings it back."

"Like get a fire ready for him to cook the meat?" said Nathan.

"That's a great idea," said Aria. "Jacob, where do you usually cook?" she asked.

"We made a fire ring at the last camp," said

Jacob. "But no one has built one here because there's nothing to cook."

"Can you show us how to make a fire ring?" asked Aria.

"Sure!" said Jacob. "We need some rocks."

"That shouldn't be hard," said Nathan. "This whole place is one big pile of rocks."

Aria giggled.

Working together, the kids found some larger rocks and rolled them into a large circle outside of camp. They stacked them until Jacob said the ring was high enough. Then Joseph went to fetch three large wooden poles. Nathan was putting the last rock into place when Laman and Lemuel walked by.

"What are you doing?" asked Laman, with a smirk on his face. "We don't have any wood to burn."

"Yes, we do," said Jacob. "And Nephi is hunting."

"You young ones are wasting your time. Nephi was hunting yesterday too," said Lemuel. "He's not going to find anything in this wilderness."

"Maybe not," said Aria. "But we think he will."

Lemuel laughed. "Okay, have fun with your rocks, kids." They laughed as they walked away.

"What is *their* problem?" asked Nathan.

"They didn't want to leave Jerusalem," said Jacob sadly. "I've never been there, but they say it was great. We had a really big house and as much food as we wanted."

"Nephi says it will be destroyed, though," said Joseph.

"I think Nephi is right," said Aria.

"Don't worry about them," said Nathan. "Let's build this fire pit before Nephi returns!"

In the middle of the ring of rocks, Jacob

showed them how to balance the three poles so they could hold meat over the middle of the fire. They bound the sticks together with lacing at the top and piled the firewood next to the ring. Aria stood back to survey their work and almost stepped on something. She bent down to pick it up. It was one of the arrows they had made with Nephi. She held the arrow, wondering what to do with it. She decided to save it for Nephi when he returned.

When they were finished with the fire ring, Nathan sat down and pulled out the camel lump he had been carving at Cub Scouts. "Cool!" said Joseph. "What is it?"

"It's supposed to be a camel," said Nathan, scowling at the wood.

Jacob snickered. "Maybe Adi will pose for you." He pointed to a camel tied up by the tent.

Joseph moved closer, looking at Nathan's

work. "It's not bad," he said. "You just need to make her head flatter—and see? Her lower lip sticks out."

"Yeah," said Nathan, eyeing the real camel's head. "You're right." He kept working. A little while later, the lump was looking more like Adi.

Aria carried the last bundle of firewood to the new pit as Nephi's wife came to see what they were doing.

"Did you build a fire pit?" she asked.

Aria nodded. "For Nephi, when he returns from hunting."

Huldah smiled, and her eyes shone. "What faith you have, little ones. He will be proud of you." She shielded her eyes, looking toward the mountain. The sun was setting now, hanging just above the horizon. "I think he may be coming."

7

IBEX FEAST

The children turned to look. A silhouette was visible in the distance, moving slowly toward camp.

"He's carrying something!" said Nathan. "Something big!"

They ran to meet Nephi, with Joseph and Jacob shouting their war cries.

When they got closer, Nephi called out to them. "Hello!" he called. "Look what I have!"

His face and hands were filthy and streaked with blood, but over his shoulder he carried the carcass of some type of deer. Aria tried not to look at the dead animal. She knew they needed it to feed all these hungry people, but it still seemed sad to kill something.

"What is it?" asked Joseph, dancing around his older brother.

"It's dinner," said Nephi with a smile. "But it *was* an ibex."

Nephi's wife greeted him with a kiss on his dirty cheek. "It's enough to feed the whole camp," she said.

Nephi nodded. "Even my grumpy older brothers."

"Wait until you see what these children have done," said Nephi's wife. "They knew you would return with meat tonight."

When they got into camp, Huldah helped Nephi prepare the meat and load it onto spits. When Nephi had washed up, Jacob pulled Nephi toward the fire pit. "Look!" he said. "Look what we did while you were gone!"

Nephi smiled at the children, his eyes shining. "I'm proud of you! You found an important way to help," he said. "It is one thing to believe, but another to act on your faith."

Nephi began stacking the wood into the fire pit. Together they built a fire in the ring and when it had burned down a bit, they set the meat to roast over the flames. As the heat of the fire slowly cooked the meat, people in the camp came out to see what was happening.

"What is that smell?" asked one woman.

"Is it really food?" cried another.

The news of the successful hunt spread quickly through the camp, and soon everyone had gathered around the fire as night descended and the flames burned brightly in the darkness. The men wore loose flowing robes and fabric bound around their heads. The women wore brightly embroidered dresses and scarves. They all looked dirty, tired, and hungry.

Laman and Lemuel appeared, looking sheepish. "I can't believe it," said Lemuel.

"Good job, brother," said Laman grudgingly.

"It wasn't my work," said Nephi. "The Lord showed me where to go."

Laman shrugged and eyed the meat eagerly.

Lehi joined them, placing his arm around Nephi. "The Lord has provided once again," he said. "Thank you for reminding us to have faith, Nephi."

Nephi placed his arm around his father's shoulder and drew his wife close on the other side. Aria watched the love on his face and found herself missing her own family. She scooted closer to Nathan. "Do you think Mom is making dinner at home?" she asked.

"Not like this!" said Nathan with a grin.

"We need to give thanks to the Lord for saving us once more," said Lehi. Everyone closed their eyes as Lehi said a prayer, thanking the

Lord for his guidance and protection in the wilderness.

The meat sizzled and hissed over the flames. When it was brown and smoking, Nephi pulled it from the fire and began to cut it into pieces. He gave the first serving to his wife and the next to his father. People crowded around, waiting eagerly for the food. Little children whimpered with hunger. Nephi cut more meat and came toward Nathan, Aria, Jacob, and Joseph. "This is for you," he said. "For all your hard work and help."

"I'm starving!" said Jacob.

"Me too!" said Joseph, stuffing a piece of meat into his mouth. Aria was hungry, but she knew more food would be waiting for her at home. She put a piece of the smoking meat into her mouth. It was warm and delicious.

"Mmm," said Nathan, chewing slowly. "Tastes like barbecue."

"Don't eat too much," said Aria. Nathan nodded.

As people finished eating, their faces shone with contentment and happiness around the fire. The night deepened, and someone began to sing. Their voices joined together in a beautiful melody rising into the night sky.

Aria listened to their song and started to yawn. She realized that she was really sleepy. "We'd better go," said Aria, turning to Nathan. She looked at her brother, but his eyes were closed. He had curled up right on the ground and gone to sleep! Aria wondered what to do.

Suddenly Nephi stood beside her. "Did your brother fall asleep? You've had a long day. There is plenty of room in our tent for both of you," he said. "Follow me."

Aria thought about protesting, but the thought of climbing the mountain in the dark to look for the enchanted tunnel didn't sound very appealing. "Okay," she said.

Nephi gently lifted Nathan in his arms and carried him to his tent. Aria followed him inside. It was completely dark, but Nephi guided her to one corner where some blankets were on the floor. "You and your brother can sleep here. My wife and I will be on the other side if you need anything."

"Thank you," said Aria. She lay down close to Nathan and curled up among the blankets. The darkness was warm and cozy. She could hear the gentle crackle of the fire and the murmur of voices from outside like a lullaby. Within a few minutes she was dreaming.

8

NEPHI'S TENT

The next morning Aria was awakened by the sound of Nathan's voice. "Wha—what? Where are we?" he said, sitting up and shaking his head.

Aria stretched and rolled over to look at her brother. "You're in Nephi's tent, silly. You fell asleep next to the fire."

Nathan rubbed his eyes. "We'd better get home!" he said.

"Yeah," said Aria. She looked around the tent. The walls were made of coarse woven fabric in many different colors and patterns. Even the ground was lined with coverings. Blankets and pillows made spaces for sitting and sleeping. It was actually much more comfortable than she would have guessed from the outside. "This is my kind of camping," said Aria.

"Way better than a regular tent," Nathan agreed.

Huldah lifted the flap of the tent. "I thought I heard voices," she said. "Good morning! Nephi is helping his father right now, but he said he can walk you to your family's camp later if you like."

"That's okay," said Aria. "We know the way." She pulled Nathan to his feet. "Our mom might be worried."

Huldah smiled understandingly. "Thank you for your help, little ones."

They said good-bye to Huldah and went to find Jacob and Joseph. They were outside, crouching on the side of the fire pit, pretending to shoot arrows at an imaginary enemy.

Aria laughed. "Hunting again?" she asked.

Joseph grinned at Aria. "Yeah," said Jacob, taking aim.

"We have to go now," said Aria.

"Aww," said Jacob. "Can you come play again tomorrow?" he asked.

Aria bit her lip. "Probably not, but we had lots of fun!"

"Yeah, it was great!" said Nathan.

The twins waved good-bye to Joseph and Jacob and to the others in camp. "Bye!" said Joseph.

"Don't forget how to war cry!" said Jacob.

"We won't," said Nathan.

As they turned to go, Nathan felt something touch his back. "Hey," he said, turning around, where he found Jacob holding something in his hand. It was one of the arrows they had made.

"You might need it out there in the desert!" said Jacob.

"Thanks!" called Nathan. He handed the arrow to Aria. "For your collection," he said.

Aria beamed. She had brought something back from every other tunnel adventure so far and couldn't wait to add this to the others.

Aria and Nathan headed back toward the mountain. The morning sun was just as bright as it had been the day before. "It's going to be another long, hot day in the desert!" said Aria.

"I'm starving," said Nathan. "That meat was great, but I'd get sick of eating it every day!"

"Me too," said Aria.

They climbed to the spot near the acacia trees and searched until they found the opening in the rock. Nathan unzipped his scripture bag and pulled out the faded pioneer bonnet. Aria tied the bonnet on her head, and they knelt down in the tunnel.

Zing! She felt the familiar sizzle of electricity move across the ground. "Let's go!" said

Nathan. They crawled forward over the rocks, trying not to scrape their hands and knees. After a few minutes the rocks became smooth. The square of light that was the opening to the cupboard door appeared in the distance and they crawled toward it. Pushing it open, they tumbled into the church gym.

9

"WHAT'S FOR DINNER?"

Just then the door to the gym flew open and two Scouts ran inside. "I'm gonna get you!" shouted Ben.

"Oh, yeah?" shouted another Scout named Ian. "Come and try! Nah-nah-nah-nah."

They started running for the stage and stopped short when they saw Nathan and Aria on the floor in dusty costumes.

"Nathan and Aria?" said Ben.

"What are you doing?" asked Ian.

Nathan and Aria looked at each other. Nathan took a deep breath. He decided to tell the truth. "We found an enchanted tunnel," he said.

"Yeah, right." said Ian. He looked skeptically at their costumes.

Aria looked shocked at Nathan's response, but smiled and added, "We just escaped from a desert hunting party!"

"Check out this arrow!" said Nathan. Aria held up the arrow Jacob had given them.

"Wow," said Ben.

"Cool!" said Ian, looking impressed. "Where did you get it? Can you help us make one of those?"

"Sure," said Nathan, smiling at Aria. Nathan's stomach rumbled loudly. "But we'll have to do it later," he said. "Right now we have to get home for dinner."

"Aww . . . okay," said Ben.

"Promise?" asked Ian.

"Yeah," Nathan agreed.

"Let's go," called Aria. They said good-bye to their friends, ran to the restrooms, quickly changed into their regular clothes, and set off for home.

As they raced across the parking lot into the darkening night, Nathan called, "Hey, Aria, do you want to set up the tent in the backyard tomorrow and pretend we're Jacob and Joseph?"

"Yeah!" said Aria. "But you will have to teach me how to do the war cries!"

Their laughter led them all the way home and gathered them around the dinner table where their mom had made a delicious dinner. She welcomed them with a hug. Aria remembered the love she had felt with Nephi's family. She felt it right here with her own family too.

"I have a surprise for you two," Mom said. "We're having barbecued beef for dinner!"

Nathan and Aria looked at each other and giggled.

"That sounds great, Mom!" Aria said, trying not to laugh.

EPILOGUE

The story of Nephi and the broken bow appears in 1 Nephi chapter 16. Scholars are not sure exactly what route Lehi and his family followed, but some LDS scholars believe they may have traveled along the border of the Arabian Peninsula, following the coast of the Red Sea. This route was a common one in Nephi's time and was known as the "Incense Trail" since spices were traded and sold along this route.

Shortly after finding the Liahona, Lehi and his family camped in a place called Shazer. From there they continued into the wilderness. After making camp, Nephi and his brothers went hunting to find food. When Nephi's steel bow was broken, Nephi's brothers were angry. They were probably greatly afraid. Lehi seems to have been quite wealthy in Jerusalem, and Laman and Lemuel would have been raised expecting to inherit their father's riches. When he instead was called to be a prophet and led them into the desert, they would have been thrown into a life they did not desire nor expect. The adjustment to life in the desert would not have been easy, as the Arabian Peninsula is a dry and desolate land in most places, and they faced dangers such as marauding armies, dehydration, scorpions, snakes, and fierce sandstorms.

After Nephi broke his bow of steel, even Lehi himself complained. However, Nephi chose to have faith and trust that the Lord would provide for them. After making a new bow from wood, he sought his father's guidance to know where to go to find food. Nephi's example humbled Lehi, who repented and sought to know the Lord's will.

After consulting the Liahona, Lehi began to tremble when he saw the writing that explained the compass worked according to their faith. Like the promptings of the Holy Ghost in our own lives, the Liahona would lead them as long as they obeyed.

Nephi was instructed to seek food at the "top of the mountain," which is often a symbol of the temple in the scriptures (1 Nephi 16:30). There he was able to slay wild beasts to feed his family. When he returned with the food, his family rejoiced and realized that the Lord had once again provided for them in the wilderness.

FUN FACTS

Jerusalem: Nephi lived in Jerusalem around 590 B.C. That means that he might have been there when the prophet Jeremiah was prophesying. The prophets Daniel and Ezekiel may have been young children at the time—perhaps they played together in the city!

Metalworking: Some LDS scholars believe that Nephi may have been apprenticed to a metalworker when in Jerusalem. In the scriptures, Nephi describes the sword of Laban with admiration and notices the fine metalwork on the Liahona (see articles listed under "To Learn More").

Sacrifices: As they wandered in the wilderness, Lehi and his family built altars and offered sacrifices. This was a way of giving thanks to the Lord for his protection. Sacrifices were symbolic of the Atonement of Jesus. Today the sacrament is also prepared on something that looks like an altar (the sacrament table) to remind us of these ancient sacrifices.

Nephi's wife: Nephi's wife is never named in the Book of Mormon, but the name Huldah was a common Hebrew name and is the name of a prophetess from the Old Testament.

Ibexes: The Book of Mormon does not say what type of meat Nephi returned with, but ibexes are wild mountain goats with long, graceful horns that live in the mountains of Israel and surrounding countries.

Tents: The tents they used in the wilderness were probably very similar to the tents still used by Bedouins in the Arabian Peninsula today. These tents are woven from camel hair, so they are very sturdy. The fibers are woven on looms into long sheets that are then sewn together to cover the tents. The inside of these tents are often filled with pillows and blankets and are very comfortable! The Bedouins are known for their brightly embroidered dresses and scarves.

Traveling in the wilderness: Nephi said they traveled in the desert for eight years before they reached the land of Bountiful. Somewhere during this time, Nephi's younger brothers Joseph and Jacob were born. The scriptures do not say how old they were at the time Nephi broke his bow.

Bountiful: The land of Bountiful may be the Wadi Saye area of Dhofar in modern-day Oman. Surrounded by desolate desert, this area is surprisingly green and lush. It is a place where fruits and vegetables grow abundantly, and it would have been a welcome change from the desert.

TO LEARN MORE

You can learn more about Nephi and other Book of Mormon prophets by looking at these additional materials:

Book of Mormon Stories (Salt Lake City: The Church of Jesus Christ of Latter-day Saints, 1997).

The Little Book of Book of Mormon Evidences by John Hilton III (Salt Lake City: Deseret Book, 2007).

Journey of Faith, a DVD produced and directed by Peter Johnson for the Neal A. Maxwell Institute of Religious Scholarship, Brigham Young University, and Timpanogos Entertainment (2006). This movie was filmed on location in Arabia and features gospel scholars discussing the journey that Lehi and Sariah and their family might have followed.

"Lehi's House at Jerusalem and the Land of His Inheritance," by Jeffrey R. Chadwick. The scholarly article talks about Nephi's childhood in Jerusalem and his experience with metalworking. View at http://maxwellinstitute.byu .edu/publications/books/?bookid=2&chapid=3; accessed 13 January 2011.

HOW TO MAKE AN ARROW

Warning:

Arrows can be dangerous. Never point a bow and arrow at someone. Before you make an arrow, ask your mom or dad for help and permission first.

What you need:

A straight stick or dowel rod
An arrowhead or a small, pointy rock
Hot glue, wood glue, or rubber cement
Thread or sturdy string
Feathers
Paint (optional)

What you do:

Step 1: If you are using a stick, you will need to scrape off the bark and sand it until it is smooth and straight. Dowel rods are available at craft stores and building supply stores, and are already smooth and straight.

Step 2: Cut a shallow notch at one end of the stick with a knife. Make sure an adult helps you with this step and always cut away from yourself! Cut a deeper notch (3/8 to 5/8 inch) at the other end. This is where the arrowhead will go.

Step 3: If you are using a small pointy rock, use another sharp rock to notch it on both sides (this is where the string will go to hold it on). Arrowheads are also available at rock and hobby shops as well as many toy stores.

Step 4: Put a small dot of glue at the end of the arrowhead and place it into the deep notch on the dowel rod or stick. Then wrap the notched end of the arrowhead tightly with a piece of thread or string 8–10 inches long.

Tie a knot at the end and finish the ends with a dot of glue. In Nephi's time, cordage made from animal tendons would have been used instead of string.

Step 5: Split feathers down the middle using scissors or a pocket knife and trim them to size. Glue three half-feathers around the end of the arrow, spacing them evenly around the wood. Wrap more thread around each end of the feathers and set the arrow aside to dry.

Step 6: When the arrow is dry, it is ready for painting, if you want. When you are finished, you can use it with a bow either to shoot at targets or to display in your room.

ABOUT THE AUTHOR

Marianne Monson spent much of her childhood looking for magic passageways. Reading good books has always been one of her favorite adventures. She studied English at Brigham Young University and also spent a semester in Jerusalem, where she walked through Hezekiah's Tunnel. Now, she particularly enjoys following her children, Nathan and Aria, as they discover their own enchanted tunnels.

Marianne holds an MFA from Vermont College in writing for children and young adults. She teaches creative writing at Portland Community College and serves as a Gospel Doctrine teacher in her ward in Hillsboro, Oregon. You can visit her at www.mariannemonson.com.